Where Would I Be in an Evergreen Tree?

Jennifer Blomgren

Illustrated by Andrea Gabriel

SASQUATCH BOOKS
SEATTLE

Acknowledgment and thanks to
the Sequim Audubon Society and Kristi Knowles,
Gino, my wonderfully supportive family and friends,
and especially Andrea.
To George.

—Jennifer Blomgren

For my wonderful family.
Your support and enthusiasm always amaze me.

— Andrea Gabriel

Printed in China
Published by Sasquatch Books
Distributed by Publishers Group West
12 11 10 09 08 07 06 05 04   6 5 4 3 2 1

Book design: Karen Schober / Bill Quinby
Interior composition: Bill Quinby

Library of Congress Cataloging-in-Publication Data
Blomgren, Jennifer.
     Where would I be in an evergreen tree? / Jennifer Blomgren ; illustrated by Andrea Gabriel.
         p. cm.
     ISBN 1-57061-414-8
         1. Forest ecology—Juvenile literature. 2. Conifers—Ecology—Juvenile literature.
         I. Gabriel, Andrea, ill. II. Title.
     QH541.5.F6B59 2004
     577.3—dc22   2004048128

Also by Jennifer Blomgren, illustrated by Andrea Gabriel, and available from Sasquatch Books: *Where Do I Sleep?*
A Pacific Northwest Lullaby. Order toll-free, 800-775-0817, or visit us at www.sasquatchbooks.com.

SASQUATCH BOOKS
119 South Main Street, Suite 400
Seattle, WA 98104
(206) 467-4300
custserv@sasquatchbooks.com
www.sasquatchbooks.com

A long time ago, on a big mossy log,
on the floor of a forest all covered in fog,
a seed from a cone fell onto the wood
and reached for the sun just as fast as it could.

Its tender young needles sparkled with dew,
like jewels in the wind, as the baby tree grew.
Its slender young trunk, so supple and small,
would someday be over two hundred feet tall.

Centuries came and centuries went.
Mighty storms blew and great branches bent.
And always the tree headed up to the sky,
to the gray misty clouds where the bald eagles fly.

The tree gave a home to hundreds of plants
and beetles, birds, butterflies, spiders, and ants.
With each passing year, more species came—
so many that some still don't have a name.

We'll show just a few who live in the tree.
We can't show them all, or this book would be
very enormous!—too big for your lap, and
too long to read without taking a nap.

Under our fir's roots, a nurse log once lay.
The hollow it left is a bear den today.
The great branches keep off the rain and the snow
that swirl far above as the bears sleep below.

The Indian pipe with its pale ghostly white
is fed by the tree roots and needs little light.
It springs from deep duff, a rich, lofty rug
full of insects and mushrooms, dead needles and slugs.

Van Dyke's salamander lays eggs on a log
that lies near our fir in this forest of fog.
A vast web of life where, when conifers fall,
they don't really die, but give new life to all.

Lovely wildflowers nod under the trees,
stirred by the fragrant and gentle spring breeze.
Trillium, shooting star, harebell, twinflower
dance to the rustling wind by the hour.

Herds of cow elk keep the green meadows clear,
helped by the smaller and shy black-tailed deer.
They browse huckleberry and all kinds of brush,
crossing wild rivers that murmur and rush.

A little brown creeper circles the tree
climbing in spirals as quick as can be.
When he reaches the top, he drops to the floor
and starts up the next tree to circle some more.

The red-breasted nuthatch has very strong feet.
He strides down the tree without missing a beat,
eating bugs as he goes, his head facing down,
like a wee locomotive, straight to the ground.

A silver-haired bat scoots beneath a bark flap,
tucked next to the trunk for an afternoon nap.
He has special sonar that helps him to fly
through a forest so dense tree limbs shut out the sky.

Lichens and mosses, so soft and so thick,
soak up the fog and the rain like a wick.
They give water back to the tree when it's dry
from their home on its branches, so high in the sky.

On a soft mossy mat, on a limb high and wide,
under spreading green boughs, marbled murrelets hide.
Cool salt air blows in from the ocean nearby
'round the home of these seabirds so quiet and shy.

See the pine marten—you'd think she could fly
way up in the treetops like birds in the sky.
With her long bushy tail and lustrous fur coat,
she sails with the wind, seeming to float.

The spotted owl hears the tiniest sound,
like the delicate footsteps of mice on soft ground.
In the deepest of woods, in the blackness of night,
she veers through the branches in soft silent flight.

Carried aloft by the cool fragrant breeze,
the flying squirrel glides through the crowns of the trees.
On the tree trunk at night he goes scurrying down
to feast on the truffles that spring from the ground.

The wings of the snowy pine-white butterflies
quietly flit in late summer's blue skies.
Flying home to the uppermost boughs, they touch down
where the sweet sun-filled air meets the canopy's crown.

So many creatures live in these woods—
In one single tree, there are more neighborhoods
than you'd find in a city, or any big town.
Some live in the canopy, some underground.
Some live in the needles, some under the bark.
Some sleep in the day and some sleep when it's dark.

There are many too many to fit in this book,
so come to the forest and quietly look.